The Tale Of
Nu

The Tale Of Nu

Linh Giako

Copyright © 2017 Han Giakonoski.

All rights reserved. No part of this book may be used or reproduced by any means, graphic, electronic, or mechanical, including photocopying, recording, taping or by any information storage retrieval system without the written permission of the author except in the case of brief quotations embodied in critical articles and reviews.

Archway Publishing books may be ordered through booksellers or by contacting:

Archway Publishing
1663 Liberty Drive
Bloomington, IN 47403
www.archwaypublishing.com
1 (888) 242-5904

Because of the dynamic nature of the Internet, any web addresses or links contained in this book may have changed since publication and may no longer be valid. The views expressed in this work are solely those of the author and do not necessarily reflect the views of the publisher, and the publisher hereby disclaims any responsibility for them.

Any people depicted in stock imagery provided by Thinkstock are models, and such images are being used for illustrative purposes only. Certain stock imagery © Thinkstock.

ISBN: 978-1-4808-4312-7 (sc)
ISBN: 978-1-4808-4310-3 (hc)
ISBN: 978-1-4808-4311-0 (e)

Library of Congress Control Number: 2017902612

Print information available on the last page.

Archway Publishing rev. date: 2/23/2017

Contents

After the Storm 1
How It All Began 4
Adoption 8
The Pups 12
The Grandparents and Their Lessons 16
Education Begins 21
The First Spring 22
Discoveries 26
One Last Good-bye 36
The Journey Begins 40
The Great Canine in the Sky 48
Island Hopping Aleutian Style 50
Island Hopping Aleutian Style Part 2 56
Divine Intervention 59
Island hopping Aleutian-Style Continues 61
On Solid Ground Once Again 67
Yukon Bound 79
The Ride 82
Moving Real Fast 86
Almost There! 90
River Crossing 92
The Land of Endless Doggie Biscuits 97

After the Storm

It was a night that no one would ever forget. All of the village people were on the north harbor jetty looking south. It was a spectacle never seen before. The whole southern sky was lit up by the remnants of a typhoon that just recently had been downgraded to a tropical storm. Constant lightning strikes made the night sky look as if it were daytime. Strong breezes were whipping up the waves and crashing against the southern jetty. With sea foam spraying everywhere and the lightning in the background, the villagers were looking at one eerie but beautiful scene.

"Have you ever seen something like that?" yelled a man standing next to Yuri's father. "This is so beautiful!"

Yuri's dad answered, "Yes, it is. Yet I am so glad this harbor has protection because this storm would have destroyed our fishing boats without it."

"You're right. You're right," agreed the villager.

Yuri and his little sister, Zoya, watched the spectacle quietly. Yuri had his hands tight against his dog's neck as if the dog would protect him from the storm.

Their dad looked down on them. "Little ones, are you scared?" Yuri and Zoya shook their heads, trying to assure their father that everything was all right.

Still, Yuri would not let go of his dog Maya. It was understandable that Yuri would seek Maya's protection. Maya was a large dog, a mix of borzoi and Siberian husky. She was fiercely loyal and protective of her human family.

After watching the lightning spectacle for a while, the father told his family that they should go back to their house because, as he put it, it was way past his bedtime. He was a baker who made all of the bread for the whole village with the help of his wife. The couple got up every morning before three o'clock to prepare the dough and bake the bread. In their village everyone was up by five o'clock in the morning, and the bread was fresh, waiting for them. Children stayed in bed for a bit longer. School didn't start until seven.

Every morning after Yuri and Zoya went to school, Maya would head to the beach to look for goodies that the ocean had washed up on the shore the night before. This morning was no different. The kids went to school, and Maya went to the beach. Because of the storm from the night before, the sea was exceptionally generous. There were all kinds of crabs, little fish, and shellfish up and down the shoreline. This morning Maya didn't have to work as hard as usual. The seagulls were the only competition for the plentiful food, and they weren't eager to share with any other creature. They dove on Maya, trying to scare her off the beach.

Maya, the village's top dog, wasn't easily scared by anything, let alone seagulls. She never understood why seagulls were so greedy and selfish. There was enough food for everyone for days to come. Besides, the bright sun felt really good and she had no intention of leaving the beach anytime soon.

With her belly full, she saw a flat rock just above the sand, climbed on it, and lay down to digest the food that she had just eaten. She was looking at the sea. The waves were considerably smaller than the night before. All of a sudden, she spied something floating on top of the water. That object wasn't very big. It moved very slowly toward the shoreline. At first, she thought it was a fish or a seal, but as it was coming closer, she realized it was neither. Her curiosity became fully awake. *What is it? What could it be?* She thought.

The object was getting closer. Even though she was very interested in the approaching object, she wasn't going to lift her full tummy off the warm rock. Latemorning sun and warmth got the best of her, and she fell asleep.

How It All Began

Maya had a pleasant dream. She dreamed that she was lying in the shade on the beachfront while full of her favorite food: whole salmon fish with roe. When her best friends Yuri and Zoya brought her the roe and cups of freshly squeezed goat milk - it was irresistible.

A large noise coming from the sea woke her up and brought her back to reality. She opened her eyes fast enough to see a large wave breaking down right in front of her. *It's nothing dangerous,* she thought. Her ears relaxed, and her eyelids closed as she tried to catch the dream again. But the dream would not come back.

All of a sudden, she felt she was very thirsty. Grudgingly, she realized she had to get up and go back to the village since there was no drinkable water anywhere near. She stood up from her warm rock and stretched for a while. Before running back to the village, she took one last look at the sea and the beach. Then she remembered the creature that was in the water. She looked again but didn't see anything. Just the sea, and the waves crushing on the beach.

With the corner of her eye, she saw something unfamiliar far away to the right. For a moment she thought it was a big fish that had washed up on the shore. The seagulls were flying above it and were close to it but not on it, so that meant it was still alive. Her curiosity took over and defeated her thirst for water. She started heading in that direction.

As she got closer, she realized that it was the creature she'd seen swimming in the water. It wasn't a fish. Coming closer yet, it wasn't a seal either. When she was close enough, she saw fur, ears, and a tail. *What could it be?* She thought.

A few steps closer, she realized it was a large dog. The dog was still alive but not moving, clearly exhausted by his ordeal. She started circling around the resting dog. *My, oh my, that's a big dog. The biggest one I've ever seen. And it's a boy!* Her interest was definitely aroused.

Maya was the biggest dog around, and she had a lot of male suitors. They were all much smaller than her. She wasn't interested in any of them. If she was going to have a partner, she wanted someone to look up to, not down upon. The dog in front of her was definitely a contender for her heart. She thought that she should help the lying dog. She stood next to him and licked his face while whining.

The dog opened his eyes and looked at Maya. He saw Maya staring at him, perked his ears up, and tried to stand up. He immediately fell back on the sand. He hadn't regained his strength yet.

Maya went close to his face and said, "Lie down. You're safe now."

The big dog obeyed.

After a while, her curiosity took over. "Who are you? Where do you come from?"

"I am Tosa Inu. I come from the land that rose from the sea many years ago. My human friends were fishing in a large boat in the ocean. I was on that boat. My job was to protect them from all perils. We were in a big storm, trying to seek shelter when a large wave hit the boat. It broke all the windows and knocked all the doors down. It swept me off the boat as well. I tried to get back on the boat but couldn't make it. I found one of the doors on the water and climbed on it. I floated on the door for many days. Then I saw land. But the water was taking me away from it so I jumped off and swam for it. Now I'm here, but I don't see my human friends. I don't know what happened to them. I think that I have failed my job." Tosa Inu bowed his head in disgrace.

"You've done the job best you could. There is no shame in it," said Maya gently. "You're safe now, and I'm sure your human friends are safe now too. The storm is gone."

"Mr. Tosa Inu—" started Maya.

"Please call me Inu," said the big dog.

"Okay. Inu, I have an idea. You can come with me and meet with my human friends. Then we will go from there. I'm sure you'll like them as well."

Inu tried to get up but still couldn't.

"I'll tell you what we can do. I'll bring you something to eat, and it'll bring your strength back." *Poor thing must be very thirsty too.* Maya knew there was no time to waste. She ran around the beach, collecting small fish so her new friend could eat. Small crabs that seagulls left on the beach were no banquets for a big dog like Inu, but it was better than nothing. He gulped them down faster than she could gather them. Soon, he felt his strength coming back.

Inu stood up and took his first steps gingerly. With each step, he felt stronger and stronger.

Finally, he arched his back and stood on all fours in all his glory.

He is a big dog, thought Maya with a twinkle in her eyes.

They started jogging toward the village.

Adoption

The afternoon was passing fast. Yuri and Zoya were back from school. Something was wrong. Usually, Maya was home to greet them, but not today. She was nowhere to be found.

"Mom, have you seen Maya?" asked Zoya.

Her mom replied, "No, I haven't seen her all day."

"I hope she is all right," said Zoya while helping her mom cook dinner.

At that moment Yuri ran into the kitchen. "Mom! Mom! Maya is outside with another dog! And he is huge!" Yuri screeched. All three went outside into the garden. There sat Maya with her tail wagging and the most innocent look on her face. Next to her was a big brown dog, the biggest they'd ever seen before. The three humans stared at the dogs in disbelief. And the dogs stared back, their tails wagging wildly.

The Tale Of Nu

Yuri looked at the dogs with his eyes wide open. He thought. *With two dogs like these, I will be the toughest kid in the village! Nobody will touch me!* He turned to his mom, looked up at her, made the sweetest face any kid could make, and started begging :

"Mom, can we please, please keep him? He's so big he could protect the whole village from the wolves and the bears in the winter. I would feel very safe with him around. If we could keep him, both Zoya and I can have our own dog. Please Mother? Pretty please?"

Mom looked down on him silently. *That's a big dog, and he probably eats a lot too. Maya is a big dog too, yet she somehow finds her own food. Maybe she could teach the big dog how to fend for himself too!* "I'm alright with it, but we must get permission from your father. If he says yes, we keep the brown dog. He does look big and fearless. We all would be safer with him around."

When Dad finally came out of the bakery, mother and he started talking. In the beginning he had a very stern look on his face. With each word spoken, his face became more and more mellow.

Finally, he got up and went back to the bakery. Shortly afterward, he returned to the kitchen with a loaf of bread that was still hot. Everybody stared at him anxiously, waiting for his decision. He strode firmly across the kitchen to the door that led to the garden. He opened the door and stopped in his tracks. He stared at the brown dog in disbelief.

"For the love of God, that is a big dog!" he mused. "What happened here? Did a bear have a baby with a dog? He must weigh a hundred kilograms!" he turned to the kids and asked, "Are you sure you want this dog in the house?"

They both nodded their heads vigorously, saying yes again and again.

Dad turned his head toward the dogs, still unsure of the decision he had just made. Then he slowly started breaking off chunks of bread and threw them to the big dog. He laid the rest of the chunks to the front of the house and on to the blanket where Maya usually slept.

Inu looked at Maya for approval. She seemed very happy the way her human friends had invited them into the house. Inu started eating the warm bread. It was food he never had before. All he ever knew was fish. This wasn't fish, but it still tasted good. Slowly, they entered the house and settled on the blanket, leaving the floor clean of any crumbs. Instinctively, he knew this was his new home.

The next morning Inu and Maya escorted the children to school. The school kids were in awe at the sight of Inu. They asked questions about where the huge dog came from, but Yuri and Zoya didn't have answers. They just said that Maya brought him home with her.

As the sun rose up in the sky, Maya took Inu back to the beach. She taught her new partner about how to find food on the beach and in the tide pools. She showed him how to sniff the crabs and dig them out of their dens with his paws. They ran happily and freely around on the sand and enjoyed each other's company. Inu has never been around other dogs before, and Maya has never been around a dog she could respect. It was a happy union. The crab runs became a daily routine of substance and play.

It was a beautiful routine and a beautiful beginning of a happy relationship between the human family and soon expecting dog family.

The Pups

The days began getting shorter as winter approached.

Maya's belly was getting bigger and bigger. The play time on the beach started getting shorter until one morning the house became filled with the sounds of new life. Maya gave birth to six pups, five girls and one boy.

Even though they were just born, the pups were really big. Maya was exhausted from the ordeal. Inu just stared at the pups, not knowing what to do or think. Many days passed in grooming and suckling the new offspring. Eventually, they opened their eyes, and saw the new world for the first time. The villagers were ecstatic. The bakers' family promised that they would give away the pups as soon as they stopped suckling. Everybody knew that with so many new big dogs around, the village would be safe from all the predators that came to visit at night.

The Tale Of Nu

As the snow fell, Maya and Inu started taking their pups outside of their house to get them acquainted with the village and its surroundings. They showed them how to find food on the beach, climb the hills, chase rabbits and squirrels, recognize and follow tracks in the snow, and all of the other useful skills that the pups would need as they grew up.

At six weeks old the villagers started coming to the bakers' home and taking the pups to their homes. The bakers made a decision to keep the male pup for themselves. Yuri and Zoya named him Nu.

Nu was a firecracker. He loved to play, and he was mischievous. He would get inro trouble any way a person could think of. But his cute face would make it easy for people to forgive him. He was the largest of the pups. He had his father's face and shoulders and his mother's long legs. The bakers knew that he would be very big and very strong. That was why they kept him.

Of course, Maya was happy with their decision. Having one of her puppies with her was better than none. Mom and Dad taught Nu everything they knew, and he learned quickly. At three months old, he was bigger and stronger than most of the dogs in the village. Even though he was young and playful, he never took any advantage of the other village dogs. And everybody appreciated him. As the nights started getting shorter, Nu started getting curious. He wanted to know everything. Inu and Maya were happy to oblige. He would ask his dad questions like "Dad, could I be a fisherman dog like you? Dad, is being on fishing boats dangerous? Dad, is life on a fishing boat fun?" Inu answered every question Nu asked.

One morning as they foraged on the beach as usual, Inu told his son about a box that could show other worlds. His human friends would look at the box when they weren't working. One day the box showed a place far, far away. In that world all of the people loved dogs. They loved to play with them. They loved to pet them and scratch their bellies and most of all, they loved giving their dogs special treats they called doggie biscuits. Those biscuits made the dogs in the box very, very happy.

"Where is this faraway land Daddy? How do you get there?" Nu asked.

"Son, from what I understand, this world is far, far away from where the sun comes up every day." Inu said.

"If you go there, how would you know you've arrived?" Nu asked.

"Son, I'm not sure. I think that they have a symbol with lots of stars and different stipes on it" said Inu. "All I remember are the trees I saw in the box. The trees had big broad leaves, so when you see broad leaves, you have arrived in the promised land."

The next morning Inu and Maya took their pup to the hills above the village. The higher they went, the deeper the snow became. It was very hard for Inu to walk on the snow because he was a big dog. His short legs would sink into the snow, so he decided to wait at the top of the first hill. It was easier for Maya and Nu to move without Dad with them.

The Tale Of Nu

Nu enjoyed playing in the snow. Suddenly, Maya spotted a rabbit in the distance. She decided to teach her son how to catch his own food. They slowly and quietly approached the hare. When Maya decided they were close enough, she quickly sprang and gave chase. The hare was no match for Maya's long legs and speed. Soon Maya caught the hare. With the dead rabbit in her mouth, she approached Nu, who was eagerly looking at his mother.

She put the hare in front of Nu, and Nu started licking the blood off the hare's fur. Maya started biting off chunks of the hare's fur and spitting them out. Then she bit into the flesh. Nu had never seen his mom feed that way. It was exciting. Then he took few bites too. After they finished eating the rabbit, they licked each other's faces clean.

With their bellies full, Maya got an idea. She knew there was a small lake nearby. She asked Nu if he would like to do something different. He eagerly said yes, wagging his tail. They climbed the small hill and they found the frozen lake, all flat and white. Maya ran to it with Nu close by. Once on the lake, they couldn't stop their movement. They slid all over the place. When they finally stop sliding, Maya stood up and told Nu she would teach him how to walk on frozen water. It took Nu a while to learn the skill, but it was all in good fun.

As the Sun began falling down beneath the tall cone mountain, Maya suggested going to get Dad and heading home before it became too cold. All three got home before dark.

The Grandparents and Their Lessons

The next morning, as soon as the Sun came up, they escorted the children to school. Maya turned to Nu and asked him: "Would you like to meet my mom? She lives nearby, and if we go soon, we'll be there in no time." Nu was ecstatic about the idea.

"Yes. Yes. Yes!" he said while running in circles around Maya. He learned to love every opportunity to see something unusual and do something out of ordinary.

Inu was not excited at all. He knew it would be hard to keep up with Maya and Nu. "You go ahead. I'll go on to the beach to find something for my breakfast."

The fishing village was surrounded by tall cone mountains.

Maya chose the middle and ran toward it. Nu could keep up only because he was still young and was lighter than Mom. By the time the Sun was in the highest point in the sky, they reached the lone log cabin at the foot of the large cone mountain. Nu was getting a bit tired. His Mom was racing in front and started barking excitedly. The reason for her excitement was another dog that resembled his mother.

"Mom! Mom! Mom!" Maya shouted, speeding over the open meadow.

The dog by the cabin turned around, and when she saw the two approaching dogs, she started racing toward them.

"My baby! You decided to visit me!"

The two dogs reached each other, and started a gracious dance of two in the middle of the small field. The view was gorgeous. There were two animals with beautiful shiny coats, jumping up and down in the snow.

When the excitement calmed down a bit, the older dog asked Maya, "Who did you come with? Who is this handsome pup?"

"This is my son. Your grandson, Mommy," Maya answered. Nu felt compelled to approach the older dog in a submissive posture.

"Hi Grandma," Nu greeted the older dog respectfully.

The three dogs continued to celebrate for quite a bit longer.

"Mom," said Maya, "My partner and I are trying to teach Nu correctly. What could you tell him?"

Grandma stopped in her tracks and suggested: "Love,

respect and protect your human friends, especially the little ones."

"I understand Grandma. What else?" asked Nu.

"Always share the food that you catch with your human friends. That will make them happy."

The rest of the day continued with gentle play, grooming one another, and a lot of face licking. Everybody was happy. After a while, Maya decided that is was time to go back home. Maya and Nu greeted Grandma for the last time before they went back to the village.

"Come back and see me again!" shouted Grandma.

"We will! We will!" Maya shouted back as Maya and Nu began the long journey back to the village.

The next morning, as soon as they left Yuri and Zoya at school, Maya asked Nu: "Would you like to meet your grandfather?"

Nu said "Yes I do Mommy."

"Not again!" Inu growled. "You two can go ahead. I'll wait for you back here. I come from a bloodline of warrior ancestors. I am a sea faring dog. I am not a mountain climbing dog!"

Maya was trying very hard not to laugh at her partner's comment. Instead, she licked his face and whispered something that little Nu couldn't hear. Then, Mom and her son went into the morning mist.

This time the journey took them to the left cone mountain. They ran over streams and meadows and some more streams. They ran around a still frozen lake so they didn't risk a fall through the ice. They ran through woods and, up and down hills, until they reached the tall cone mountain. In the distance, they saw a strange-looking structure at the edge of the tree line. As they approached closer, they saw a large husky tied up to a pine tree. The dog was on a long leash that allowed enough movement. As Maya and Nu arrived, the dog on the leash barked, "Who are you? What do you want here?"

"Daddy. I'm your daughter, and this is your grandson. We decided to visit you," Maya said respectfully.

Nu peeked his head from behind his mom and looked at the big husky. Now he knew where his mother's hauntingly beautiful blue eyes came from.

"Hi Grandpa," greeted Nu. The big husky couldn't believe what he was seeing. Right in front of his eyes was a pup almost as big as himself.

"He is such a big pup!" he said.

"I know," Maya said coyly. "His father is a huge dog."

After they approached the big husky, they started greeting each other. Again, Nu acted respectfully. After all the greetings has ceased Maya asked her father to teach her son about the secrets of life she never knew. The big husky began sharing the secrets of running long distances.

"It's easier to run on snow," said the big husky. "If you have to run over long flat snow, keep running steady. Don't waste your time looking for food. There won't be any. You will find food only where the ground is not even, in the woods, or near water. If you hear the howl of wolves, don't stop running. Head to the opposite direction."

"What are wolves, Grandpa?" Nu asked

"Wolves are wild dogs, and they are not your friends. If you have to fight bears, jump onto their faces and bite hard on their noses. That is the only way to defeat bears," said the big wise dog. "And one more thing," he continued and then paused as if he was trying to remember what he was going to say. "If you run over frozen water, try your best not to fall in. If you do fall in, you would not like it, I assure you. And one more thing: if you must run very far, never use up all of your energy. Pace yourself!"

"Thanks Dad!" Maya said.

"Thanks Grandpa," Nu said.

They all spent some more time together until the sun started going behind the tall mountain.

"Daddy, it's time for me and my son to go home. It will be past dark before we get home." Maya said apologetically.

"Come back! Don't be strangers!" shouted the large dog.

"We'll be back, Grandpa!" promised Nu

The path back to the village was a dangerous ordeal. By the time they were halfway there, it was well into the night.

Education Begins

As they climbed the last hill before the coastline, they saw a long beam of light break the darkness. The light was moving around, cutting through the darkness like a long knife.

"Where is that light coming from, Mom?" Nu asked.

"That light is created by our human friends to invite everyone into their home," Maya answered.

"Why have I never seen that light before? Why don't our friends have it?" Nu asked.

Maya answered, "That light is hard to create. Not everyone can create it. Our friends make bread, not light."

To their left lied the village dotted with weak lights like a field full of fireflies. They headed in that direction. When they came home, Inu was fast asleep, his belly bulging full of food. Maya remembered how hungry she was; however, she was also exhausted, and she fell fast asleep.

The First Spring

The days grew longer than before. The snow was long gone, and the air was filled with the smells and sounds of spring. Flowers were blooming. Bees were busy pollinating, and the birds came back from migration. Those were happy days, the best days of Nu's life.

All the young animals were eager to play. Getting in some sort of trouble was a daily occurrence, but it was all for good. In the afternoon the village children would come back from school. On one of those occasions, Nu met with two dogs that almost looked like him. At first, he didn't realize that they were his sisters. They started talking to one another, and he learned he had three more sisters which were taken to the big city to the north.

"How did that happen?" asked Nu.

One of the sisters told them that their human friend moved them to the big city where they would have a better life.

"But, how were they taken away?" Nu questioned again.

"In a big, horseless carriage," said one of the sisters.

"What is a horseless carriage? I've never seen one," Nu asked.

"It is as big as a boat, but it goes on dry land," one of his sisters said.

"A boat?" asked Nu. "That means it doesn't run!"

"No," his other sister said, "it's more like a sled."

"Oh, I see," said Nu.

"This carriage drives on a big path. I know this because that path goes right by our house," said the sister.

"Can I go with you and see it?"

"Sure!" said one of the sisters. "Let's go!"

The three large puppies went to the north side of the village. After a while, they came to a clearing. It was filled with boxes, nets, cages, and ropes. The dogs stopped.

"See? There is a horseless carriage over there! See it?"

Nu looked at the strange object. It was big, and it stood on some wired round things. Suddenly, a human figure climbed into the box. Soon after that, a sound came from the box that made Nu jump in fear. The loud box started moving away, creating a cloud of dust and smoke. Nu was terrified because of what he saw. His sisters started chasing the box, but he couldn't move. Shortly afterward, his sisters ran back all excited.

"Why didn't you come with us? It's fun to chase after it!"

Nu didn't say anything.

"I'd like to go back home," he declared.

"Okay! We'll show you the way back!"

As they approached the familiar territory, Nu's fear was replaced by curiosity.

"Do you think we could go to the city and find our other sisters?" Nu asked.

"I guess," one sister said.

"Why not? It's not like we have something better to do!" the other sister said.

"Then we'll do it tomorrow!" said Nu. "Morning is the best time to start, so that we have time to return before the sun goes down."

"Tomorrow then," one sister said.

"See you tomorrow," said the other sister.

Each one of them went to their homes. That night, Nu went to bed early. He dreamed of bravely chasing after the horseless carriage. As he slept, his feet moved as if he were running. Maya, Inu, and all of the human friends wondered what he was dreaming about.

The next morning Maya and Inu went to escort the children to school. When they came home, Nu was nowhere to be found. Mom and Dad didn't worry too much. They knew nothing in the village could hurt him too much. He was their big pup. So they left to go forage for food on the beach.

In the meantime, Nu and his two sisters were heading north out of the village, following the long path. On many occasions, they encountered horseless carriages, and every time they had to yield to the noisy beasts.

Hours went by, and the big city was nowhere to be found.

As the sun started going down in the sky, they realized that they might not be able to find the big city and their sisters there. They had to return to the village before their families had reasons to worry about them. Nu made it home just in time to see nightfall. His mom and dad were upset with him. At that time, it didn't matter to him. He was so tired that he just collapsed on the blanket and fell asleep. Maya and Inu were perplexed.

    Nu and his sisters tried a few more time to reach the big city, but with no prevail. The big city was always out of their reach. Finally, they decided not to try any more. They came to a realization they may never see their other three sisters again.

Discoveries

The first summer of Nu's life was the summer of exploration and wonder. Wherever he looked, there was grass, trees, bushes, and flowers. All the insects appeared to be flying in completely random ways. All Nu had to do was stay still and look around, there were new and exciting things to discover. Morning foraging on the beach wasn't as plentiful. It seemed that the sea was stingier in the summer.

"Quiet water does not give many presents, my son," said Maya one morning. Still, they went to the beach every morning, sometimes with their human friends in tow. Nu enjoyed the summer walks because he was accompanied by both of his parents. He questioned them about everything. He loved listening to his father talking about past events he had heard from his father. Inu told his son about the things that happened before time even begun and about his ancestors that bravely went to war, fought, and won. There was a story of a tall mountain, whose peak was the gathering place for all of his ancestors, looking down at cherry blossoms in spring and new life during summer.

On one of those morning walks, a strange dog approached Nu and his family. That dog was neither friendly nor polite. Nu decided to engage the dog and made short work off him. The other dog ran away yelping. Nu proudly trotted back to where his parents were. He expected praise for his action. Instead, his father gave him a stern lesson.

"Pup, you didn't have to use that much force against a smaller adversary. You could have just stood there and let your size speak for you, and you didn't have to hurt it. There is no honor in fighting a smaller opponent"

Nu bowed his head and tucked his tail between his legs. "Yes Dad."

All three of them continued their foraging on the beach. The memory of the fight still fresh in Nu's mind, the little pup gathered some courage and asked his father, "Father, if that dog was much bigger, how should I have fought him?" That question stopped Inu in his tracks. He stood tall and explained to his son, "If the opponent is about your size, you bite him on the neck until they submit. If your opponent is much bigger than you, you leap and bite hard on his snout. When you crush his snout, it will take all the fight out of your opponent. If your advisory is smaller than you, a firm bit on their rump would suffice. For anything else, just stand your ground and bark loud. They will leave you alone."

"Thanks, Dad. I appreciate your teachings," said Nu.

Nu looked at Maya and stated, "That was the same thing that Grandpa told me, right Mom?"

"Yes, dear, your grandpa is quite a fighter too," said Maya proudly.

As they kept foraging, Nu asked more and more questions.

That morning their foraging took them much farther than ever before. Up in the distance, Nu saw a tall, skinny structure. He remembered his mom telling him about human friends making the fire that he saw that night. He knew his dad worked on a fishing boat before, and he asked him about the light. His dad explained to him that the lights reached really far out to warn all the boats where the land came out of the sea.

"Yes," he added, "when the lights are on, humans are always around, and they always have dogs to protect them and help them with chores. In the still of the night, sometimes you can hear them bark. That's why dogs stay near the lights and on their boats to keep their humans from danger"

That night Nu dreamed about being a lifesaving dog at the human light structure.

The next morning as they went back to the beach, one of his sisters appeared by the garden. Submissive, she approached Inu and Maya.

"It's nice to see you, Mom and Dad." Maya was ecstatic at the sight of one of her daughters.

"You came to visit us! How nice of you!"

"Yes, Mommy, I came to see you, but I also wanted to see

if my brother would like to join me and my human friends in a hunt."

"Can I go, Mom? Dad? Please?" Nu was excited.

"I don't know, babies. Hunting can be dangerous. Inu, what do you think? Should we let them go hunting?"

Inu's answer was short and straightforward. "Yes, hunting is a good skill to learn."

Nu followed his sister to her home. When they got there, the hunting party had already left. The house was empty. They easily followed the fresh scent. This time they were heading to the cone mountain to the right. Soon they caught up with the hunters. There were three humans carrying some kind of sticks. Soon, Nu's sister told him to be quiet and watch what he was stepping on. They entered a thick brush. They kept on going forward, and it seemed that they didn't have any plan until they reached a clearing in the woods. Everybody in the hunting party got very still and quiet. At the far end of the clearing, was a very large furry animal that he had never seen before. Nu started getting restless that is until a gentle bite on his rump reminded him to be quiet.

Then one of the humans raised the stick, and aimed it at the big animal. Nu saw smoke coming out, and heard a loud noise which made Nu jump up in fear. Then everybody started running at the fallen animal. When they arrived at the spot, the creature laid motionless in the tall grass.

"What happened over here?" Nu asked his sister.

His sister replied, "My human friend used his stick to

create a lightning bolt to kill this bear. This will be our food for days to come. I love to eat bear meat."

"Oh, I see," answered Nu. He wasn't sure he understood anything about what had transpired.

The humans worked fast. They cut up the animal and put it in blankets. In the meantime, they let Nu and his sister feast on the remnants of the animal. They started a fire and threw many pieces into the fire to burn it. The smell of the burnt flesh filled the whole meadow.

Everybody ate. Nu couldn't decide what tasted better: bloody meat or burnt meat. He thought, *I like them both.*

When the fire died, they all headed home. They were struggling to carry the large bags. Nu looked at his sister, "I wonder why they took us with them."

His sister replied, "There are wolves in these woods. They can hear the lightning and smell the flesh, and we are here to protect them." *Uh-huh,* thought Nu *I'm so full I don't think I could fight. I hope wolves don't come.*

The "Great Canine In The Sky" granted his wish. The wolves never showed up, and the hunting party came home safe.

As they arrived at his sister's home, Nu thanked her for inviting him to the hunting trip. He told her that he had a great time and that he'd like to go again if possible. She licked the last stains of dried blood off his face and went inside her house. Nu rushed to his home. He excitedly told his mom and dad about the hunt. He slept well that night.

The next morning Nu, his parents, and their young human

friends went to the beach. The weather was warm, and the water was calm. The ocean didn't bring any presents this morning. They ran up and down looking for food, but they didn't find anything. Nu wasn't particularly hungry. He had some food left in his stomach from the last afternoon. The human children were playing in the sand while the three dogs were sunbathing on the warm rocks nearby.

"Dad, tell me again about the box that showed other worlds!"

Inu, who almost fell asleep enjoying the warmth of the rock he was laying on and the sun above, started telling his son the story in a soft and steady manner. "When I and my human friends were not fishing, we would stay on our boat relaxing, eating, and watching the box. That box was very interesting. It showed many interesting things. One time the box showed a world that was sporting a symbol that had many stars and stripes. Humans spoke with voices I couldn't understand, and they showed many dogs going into this big house that had many toys and treats that dogs enjoyed eating and playing with. The dogs said that they were very happy when they ate some treats called dog biscuits."

"Did you ever have dog biscuits, Dad?" interrupted Nu.

"No, I only ate fish."

"How boring is it eating only fish," said Nu quietly.

"I love eating fish, Son. It's good for you," Inu responded.

All three dogs lay quietly on the warm rock. *I have to find that land that's full of dog biscuits*, thought Nu. *Seems like a happy place.* The sound of the surf and the melodic sound of the children playing on the beach enticed the three dogs into sleep under the warm sun.

The next morning, Nu asked Maya if she would allow him to visit Grandpa. She wasn't sure that he could do it. But she instinctively knew that she had to let go of her son and let him grow on his own to be his own dog.

She said, "Okay, go ahead. Are you sure you can find Grandpa's home?"

Nu was excited at the thought of going on an adventure by himself. "Yes, Mom, I remember. Look to the tall cone mountain to the left and grandpa will be there."

Before Nu could go, Maya gave him some advice, "On your way back, if you think you are lost, climb the tallest hill you can find and look around. Look for the long light shining away from you. That is where the beach is. Once you are on the beach, the village is easy to find."

Nu was excited for his adventure. He licked his mom's face, turned around, and ran toward the hills covered by thick forest. The feeling of freedom and the new adventure was something that he never had experienced before. He loved it. The challenge of navigating himself through the forest, over streams, and around lakes, was extraordinary. He ran faster than ever before, but he never felt tired. He found the left cone mountain and started running toward it.

Not long after, he arrived at his grandpa's home. Grandpa was still tied to the same tree, and his human friends were nowhere to be found

"Grandpa! Grandpa! It's me, your grandson."

The Tale Of Nu

Grandpa jumped to his feet and turned toward the dog running toward him. He definitely loved Nu's company.

"My grandson! What brought you here? Where is your mother?" the large dog asked.

"I came alone. Mom allowed me to come alone."

"How nice of you, pup."

"Grandpa! I want to ask you some questions, and I know you can teach me!"

"Go ahead, pup. I'm ready."

"Grandpa, I'll tell you a secret. My dad told me about a land far away that sports stars and stripes. Do you know of such place?"

"Yes, as a matter of fact, I do. I've been there," the big dog replied. "My human friends and I were hunting for seals. When we would get enough seals, we would take their skins off, put the skins on a sled, and take them to the faraway place you are talking about. When we got there, we would give the skins to the people who lived there. Then they would give us goodies to take back home. I have to warn you. It's a very long trip. It takes many days and nights to travel both ways."

"Could you tell me more about how to get there, Grandpa?"

"Yes, I will. First, you must travel in the winter, when the water freezes flat. You start your journey toward the rising sun, but you must be aware that the nights are very long and days are very short. The time when you see the sun rise will be very short, so you must pay attention. Next, you must run close to the water. Make sure you don't fall in. On the flat ground, don't waste your time looking for food. Third, keep looking for long lights that humans build to show the way for travelers. Where there are the lights, there are humans and food. And lastly, try to stay away from the white bears; it is hard to fight those creatures. Also, it's hard to find shelter on the flat ground."

"What about wolves, Grandpa? Are there wolves on the flat ground?"

"No, don't worry about wolves on the flat ground. They like forests and hills."

"One of my sisters showed me this wide path with large horseless carriages on them. Are there any large horseless carriages on the flat ground?"

"Well, grandson, those paths are very useful to follow. That will be the easiest and fastest way to travel and will always lead to humans. Stay on them and follow them if you find them. But no, horseless carriages don't go on flat land. In winter, the flat ground is very large frozen water. Those carriages are too heavy to travel on frozen water."

"And yes," added the big Husky, "I know the place you are talking about. I think it is much farther than the place I have been. You must travel a long way to reach that land."

"How do I know I'm there?"

"There are three things: one, it gets warmer than here. Two, wide-leaved trees live there. Three, the symbol you are telling me about will be flying high on trees without any branches."

"Thank you, Grandpa," Nu said. He loved his grandfather's wisdom, and he showed it in his farewell. He assumed a submissive posture, rubbed his head against his grandfather's side, and said his farewells.

"I'll miss you, Grandpa," Nu said.

"I'll always think of you, my grandson. Good luck."

One Last Good-bye

After his visit with his grandpa, Nu felt very confident about his trip to the promised land of endless doggie biscuits. He didn't really know when to start the trip. All he knew was that he had to wait till it was cold enough for water to freeze. As Nu gathered the courage needed for the trip, the days grew shorter, and the sea grew wilder. Storms became heaver. Every morning, the heavy fog would engulf the water, the beach, and the hills above. Yet the village fisherman kept going out fishing because this was the time when most of the fish came in from the ocean to spawn. Every morning the dogs went to the beach, and every day the sea became increasingly generous. These were the plentiful days. With so much food around, Nu grew fast. He felt restless. He discovered that he didn't like the wait. The same daily routine didn't appeal to him anymore. He wondered how his grandfather managed his life when he was chained to a tree. He decided he had to try to do something about it. He decided to go back and bring his grandpa freedom. One morning, the kids didn't go to school. It was still foggy and damp. He headed back to where his grandpa lived. As he ran away from the coastline, the fog started to dissipate. It made him feel good about finding his grandpa's cottage in the woods. As he ran, he realized the morning coolness felt good to him. Finally, he found his grandpa.

"Grandpa! Grandpa! I'm back!"

"Grandson, I'm glad you came back! I was thinking about you and your trip."

"Grandpa, would you like to join me?" Nu interrupted.

Grandpa's ears perked up and quickly went back down. "Grandson, I can't. I'm chained to this tree."

"But, Grandpa, I can help you get free!"

Nu's eagerness and honesty was evident in his body language. He really wanted his grandpa to come with him.

"This tree is too big, and these chains are unbreakable. No matter how strong you are, you can't help me pup."

Nu could feel his grandpa's sadness. He wanted to help so badly. He ran up and down the tree and the length of the chain that restricted his grandpa's freedom. He didn't see any weaknesses that he could exploit.

"I tell you what, my grandson. You will always be in my thoughts, and every day I will use my special howl to the "Great Canine in the Sky" to guide you and protect you on your journey." Grandpa continued, "I thought about the route you should take. Every time you see a path where the horseless carriages use, you should use it too. Always go around the human villages instead of running through them. There are lots of dangers in those strange places. Run steady, and always look for food, unless you're on flat ground. When you're on the flat ground, use your nose to sniff for food and never pass on anything. It doesn't matter how bad the food looks. It's better to eat rotting seal meat than die of starvation. And finally, only trust humans around the long lights. Those are good humans. The others might act friendly and then put chains around your neck like they did to me."

"Thanks, Grandpa. I'll remember that. But could you tell me how to get to the other side of the flat land?"

"Yes, pup. It's easy. When the snow gets heavy, and you can run on the frozen lakes, that will be the time to leave. After you pass the big settlement, start counting the long lights. When you pass the third long light, turn away from the mountains, and then just keep running. Always run in the direction of the rising sun. Stop to rest at the long lights as you go. It will take you a long time to cross over the frozen water to the other side. It will be many moons before you get there. When you see horseless carriages on the very wide paths, that will mean you have passed the flat land, and then follow the wide paths in the direction of the sun. They will take you where you want to go. And be careful. The journey will be perilous."

"Thank you, Grandpa. I will always remember you and your words. I still wish you could come with me."

"Me too, pup. Me too," the large Husky said softly. Go now. It'll start getting dark soon."

They touched noses. Nu took a submissive posture. "Good night, Grandpa. I will always miss you."

The big Husky turned his head away. "Go now, pup. Go." He didn't want his grandson to see his sadness.

"Thanks for everything, Grandpa!" Nu shouted as he sprinted for the shoreline.

He arrived home without any problems.

The Journey Begins

The cold weather was getting a grip on the village and the coast line. An occasional snowflake would remind everyone of winter's fast approach. Nu wanted to say his good-byes to his grandma, but for some reason, he didn't do it. Instead, he decided to check out the lake in the hills. *It's going to be a short trip*, Nu thought. Up in the hills, all the trees had lost their foliage. The nature was preparing for winter. Nu saw the lake, and it seemed that it was frozen solid. It was a sign that it was time to begin his journey.

The next morning, he went with his mom and dad to the beach to forage for food. He wanted to tell them about the trip, but somehow he didn't have enough courage to tell them. They all went home without Nu saying a thing to anyone.

A few more days went by. It was all the same routine : escort the children to school, go foraging on the beach, and maybe play a little. At last, on a day when the children didn't go to school, Nu decided to leave. He played with the children for a bit, and then he went to his mom. His mother was exploring things in the garden. He didn't say anything to her. He just looked at her beautiful face. He looked at his dad as he lay relaxing at the top of the stairs. Then his dad got up and put some chunks of bread in front of Nu. Even though Nu wasn't hungry, he still appreciated the gesture. He ate little bit to please his father. Then, he left, never to see his family or his human friends again. There were some village dogs that invited him to play, but he ignored them and kept running.

Soon he came up on to the wide path. It was empty and quiet. He kept on running. At the top of the first hill, he stopped, turned around, and took a last look at the village he grew up in. The fog was lifting, so he had a pretty good view. He felt sad. Then he thought about the journey ahead, and he continued running.

He spent the whole day running away from his village. He remembered his grandfather's advice and paced himself. He encountered very few horseless carriages. He wisely yielded to them. It was getting dark quickly. His surroundings were completely unfamiliar. He started feeling tired. He realized that he should have looked for shelter sooner. The path was running next to the seashore. He could hear the waves crashing against the rocky beach. He knew he wouldn't find any shelter on that side, so he crossed over to the other side of the wide path. He searched for anything that he could sleep in. Suddenly, he spotted a fallen tree. He decided to spend the night there. He chose the spot where the biggest branch was still attached to the tree. That was a good spot that would protect him from the cold wind at night.

That was the roughest night of his young life. Not only it was damp and cold, but those horseless carriages kept him awake all night. The shelter was right beside the path they rode on.

At the first crack of dawn, Nu got up, shook his body, and stretched his aching legs and back. The fog was still on the ground. He couldn't see the ocean, but he could hear the waves crashing. Nu went down to the shore and scavenged for food to eat. Soon, it was time to travel. The fog lifted. At least he could see the carriages coming and going. He pressed on. Then, he noticed something he never saw before. Far off the beach, he saw some large structures, floating on the water. He had never seen something like that before. He knew he liked discovering new things.

As the day progressed, the path he traveled on began moving away from the ocean and started climbing up and down the hills. At the end of the day, just as the sun began falling behind the cone mountains, he saw something that made him stop in his tracks. A huge village that went as far as his eyes could see. He saw the lights turning on, and everything in his view lit up, from the ocean to the mountains. To his right, the ocean was filled with large floating structures. To his left, were the three cone mountains. The sun was already behind them. Between the sea and the mountains were the lights, more lights than he had ever seen before. Nu wondered what he should do next. He remembered his grandpa's advice. *Don't run into any place that has many humans.* Nu decided to find a shelter before the night fell. From the top of a hill, Nu spotted a house that seemed to be empty, and he headed in that direction. Nu was right. The house was empty, and he made himself at home.

    The morning sun rays cutting through the windows woke Nu. Even though the house was cold, he felt much better. He was dry and well rested, and he would need that. Nu searched around the house for something to eat. He couldn't find anything. Then he went outside, he realized there was nothing there either. Nu then decided to move on. He ran over the path, through orchards, through people's yards, trying to stay away from humans, and if he found any scraps, Nu would take advantage of the opportunity. It took him a whole day to get to the coast on the other side of the large village. He found an empty barn, and he took shelter in it. Nu buried himself in the hay to keep himself warm and fell fast asleep. In the morning he managed to catch a rat for breakfast. Then Nu caught another one. The whole barn was crawling with rodents. Outside of the barn, there was a stream, Nu enjoyed the fresh drink.

    He kept running, making sure he never strayed too far from the sea. There were no more paths to follow. It became his daily routine searching for food and shelter while staying close to the sea and going in one direction. The progress was slow. Sometimes he would not eat for days. After all these days, Nu hadn't seen any of the long lights that his grandfather had described. Nu didn't doubt his grandpa. He just kept searching and kept his spirits high. He was very sure that his grandfather gave him the correct directions. He just had to follow them. The nights and the days were similar with fog at night and early morning or rain when the sun was up. It was getting harder to find food. The cold and wet weather kept every creature in their well-hidden shelters.

Finally after many days, the weather broke. The sun was up all day. Nu spent most of the day enjoying the warmth of the sun. He came upon long sandy beach. He knew how to find fresh food in this environment. With his belly full, he had to slow down a bit. The beautiful day was ending. Nu finally saw the moon for the first time in many nights. Nu decided to keep moving on longer because he could see well in the moonlight. Then he picked up the scent of a rabbit and started following it. It had been a long time since he had eaten a rabbit. Even though he wasn't that hungry Nu was excited about the possibility of having meat for dinner. He followed the rabbit tracks until he came upon the top of a hill, then he saw something. A long ways ahead of him, he saw a long light. Nu was very happy. Finally, there was proof that he was heading in the right direction. Nu almost felt as if he had reached his destination. He pressed onward. After he ran few miles toward the long light, he decided to find shelter and rest. That night he slept well.

When he woke up in the morning, he didn't bother foraging on the water's edge. He just ran straight to the structure with the long light. He reached it at the same time the sun reached the highest point in the sky. He expected to find nice

The Tale Of Nu

humans, friendly dogs, and perhaps some food. He found none of that. He barked and barked and scratched on the structure's door, but all to no avail. There was nobody inside. His stomach reminded him that he hadn't eaten that day. He climbed down to the water's edge, and found plentiful food in the tide pools. The rock below the long light was teeming with life that he could eat. He ate so much that he could barely climb back up to the structure. He noticed that the fog was returning. There were a lot of places to have shelter around the structure, so he decided he would spend the night there.

Just when Nu was about to fall asleep, a loud noise made him jump in bewilderment. The exceptionally loud sound disappeared for a while, but then it came back again. Nu tried to go to sleep, hoping that the noise wouldn't happen again. It did. The noise was keeping Nu awake all night. *I made a mistake by sleeping here,* thought Nu. The next morning he went back down to the beach for a quick breakfast, and then he kept running. Nu fell into a routine. He would wake up, eat the critters by the sea, start running, get lunch, keep on running, eat dinner, and then find shelter for the night, all while he looked for the next long light. One day Nu saw floating chunks of frozen water. He was curious and stopped to see if he could swim to them. Just as he put his paws into the water, he immediately pulled them back out. The water was super cold. *Bad idea, bad idea, bad idea,* Nu repeated in his mind. *Don't try to swim to those floating pieces of frozen water.* Nu kept running and running. He got so used to running that his mind began to wonder. *I wonder how my family is doing.* Nu would sometimes think.

Then all of a sudden, Nu found the next structure! This time there was a friendly human in it just as Nu's grandfather had said. "Aw, aren't you one poor stray? Here." The human threw Nu a large fish. He was grateful for the present and he enjoyed his dinner. After that he thought about staying near to regain his strength, but his memory of the loud noises told him to get away from the structure with the long lights. Since he wasn't hungry any more, he decided to stay away from the shoreline and try to run on the snow above. As he ran, he noticed many tracks in the snow. Some were strange, and some were familiar. Some went deep into the snow, while other barely left any trace. He recognized some of the snow tracks. He had seen them before. Since his belly was full, he didn't feel the need to hunt. He pressed on at a faster pace. That night he slept on the side of a big boulder. He was surprised to discover that sleeping in the snow was a bit comfortable.

During the night he heard a faint but familiar sound. He knew it was coming from the structure with the long lights. As the morning came, Nu stretched his body and shook off the snow. He felt good. Nu wasn't hungry, so he just started running. The fog stayed above him in the woods, so he could see far ahead. At midday he spotted the third skinny tall structure with the long light. This time he didn't even bother to approach it. All the time when he was running at the edge of the forests he noticed rabbit tracks and scents. He knew that he can easily catch his meals when he got hungry.

The Tale Of Nu

He continued in the same direction well above the sea shore. Next day he saw the sea began getting covered with snow and ice. It was the beginning of the flat snow. He remembered what his grandfather told him. After the third structure, he was meant to turn away from the mountains and run, so he pressed on. At this point the snow was everywhere. Everything was white. To be on the safe side, he continued northwards a bit longer. He sure didn't want to risk falling into the frigid water.

As the night was quickly approaching, Nu found some shelter between some bushes and a fallen tree. He lay there to rest. It seemed like he wasn't that tired though, so he didn't know what to do. He thought about it, but he realized that running in total darkness was dangerous. That night he rested well. At first light he decided to start running in the flat snow. Before he could reach the frozen ocean, he saw some fresh rabbit paw prints in the snow. Suddenly, he realized he was hungry. He couldn't pass up the promise of a good breakfast, so he started following the prints in the snow. He found the hare and gave chase. Soon, his breakfast was in his paws. The big hare was the last meal he had eaten in his motherland. Then he went down to the flat snow. He started running away from the mountains as his grandfather had instructed him. By sunset, he could no longer see the mountains, only the rays of the sun, which illuminated the sky with strange glow. That first night, he got lucky. The moon was bright, and he could see far in every direction. Everywhere he looked, the sky was black, and the ground was white. Nothing stood out. He pressed on.

The Great Canine in the Sky

"I see an animal running on the frozen ice. What is it?" asked The Great Canine in the Sky.

"That is a young pup from Borodin village in Kamchatka, Your Most Holiest" answered one of the Great Canine's advisors.

"A pup? That looks like a grown dog to me," The Great Canine in the Sky stated. "Anyway, where is he headed?"

"As far as I can see, it looks like he is heading to Alaska, and I haven't figured out why."

"Well, it doesn't matter why he's going there, I think we should help him," said The Great Canine in the Sky.

"How does the Great Holly of the Holiness plan to achieve that?"

"I'm putting you in charge of aiding the pup. Sometimes you can part the fog for him. Sometimes you can send the northern lights to guide him. Sometimes you can help him to find food. Sometimes you could steer him away from trouble."

"Consider it done, Your Most Holly of Holiness," said the little voice. "I'm on it right away."

Island Hopping Aleutian Style

Nu thought about trying to find a place to rest. He couldn't see anything anywhere. The clear sky indicated he was moving in the right direction. Just before dawn, he saw long lights flashing on and off. He adjusted the direction of where he was running and headed toward the lights. As the sun started peeking through the horizon, he finally saw land. The structure with the long light was right in front of him. As he approached it, he heard barking. He was very happy that he would see another dog. After a short climb, he was at the structure. He saw a dog that was restrained by chains, and it reminded him of his grandpa's fate. The chained dog was very happy to see him.

"Who are you?" the dog inquired. "Where did you come from?"

"I am from a village in the shade of the three cone shaped mountains. My human friends make delicious bread." That thought made Nu hungry.

"What are you doing here?" asked the other dog.

"I'm on a journey to the land from which the sun comes up every day."

"Where are you going?" asked the dog eagerly.

"I'm going to the land of endless doggie biscuits," Nu replied.

"I see," said the dog. The dog wondered what doggie biscuits are.

"Hey, do you know if there is anything to eat here? I'm getting hungry." asked Nu

"Well, I tell you what. My human friend went hunting for seals. When he comes back, there will be plenty of meat for me and you. You're welcome to stay and wait here with me." The dog added. "My human loves dogs."

Then the chained dog continued, "Or, I heard a big fish died on the other side of the island, and all the free animals are there feasting."

"How big is this fish?" asked Nu.

"The fish is bigger than this structure. I'm sure there will be plenty of food for many days to come."

Wow, that's a big fish, thought Nu. *I think I should stay here and wait for the human to bring seal meat and rest and enjoy the company. The land of endless doggie biscuits can wait.*

"Are you sure you don't mind if I stay?" Nu asked his new friend.

"You are very welcome to do so," said the dog, still wondering what doggie biscuits were. The dogs played, talked, and played some more. When night fell, they slept in his friend's dog house. Feeling a warm body next to him comforted Nu a lot. Nu rested well, even though he was very hungry.

Just before the sun rose, they woke up to a noise. The human friend was coming back on his little horseless carriage. It seemed like the human didn't mind the presence of the new dog. He brought two dead seals with him. Before the sun was up in the sky, the seals were chopped up. The human threw the seal intestines to the dogs. They eagerly started eating the fresh food. It smelled like rotten fish but tasted really good. Nu made quick work of his portion. He approached the human submissively and gave a little whine. He was still hungry. The human said to him, "I guess you need more food. You're a big dog." He scraped the fat from the seal skin and threw it to Nu.

My goodness, this is the best food I've ever had in my life, he thought. *This tastes better than any bread or rabbit I've ever had!* The fat meal gave him a lot of energy.

"I feel like I could run for days and days!" he said to the dog.

"Stick around! We'll get all the seal fat. My human likes the meat," responded his friend.

Why not? Nu thought. *This dog seems to know how to live.* The two dogs spent the whole day together, playing and eating.

I feel great! Nu thought.

The Tale Of Nu

"Seal fat makes you feel strong and really great, doesn't it?" asked Nu's friend. It was like he read Nu's mind.

"Yes, indeed."

Nu spent another day at the long light structure. *I'll continue in the morning,* Nu thought to himself.

After the third sunrise, Nu said good-bye to his friend. "I have to go. Thank you for your hospitality. I will never forget you."

"Likewise," said his friend.

"Can you tell me again which way you go to get to the dead fish?" asked Nu one last time.

"I heard it's on the other side of the island. Just stay on the sunny side. You'll get there. You can't miss it. Be careful of the bears. That place will be crawling with bears. They are very dangerous and very big, much bigger than you. May the Dog Gods be with you."

He ran all day, and as the night began to fall, he caught a strange scent. It was a concoction of many things but mostly rot. As he quickly approached, the scent got stronger. Finally, up in the distance, he saw a small round hill. Part of it was covered with snow. Then he realized *it* was the dead fish. He has never seen anything like that in his life. Around the giant fish were little humps. He ran to the fish. He couldn't resist the promise of that much food. He tore into the carcass, swallowing chunks of blubber. He heard some grumbling, but he didn't pay much attention. Suddenly, out of the corner of his eye, he saw something moving. It was a giant white bear staring at him. Nu's heart skipped a beat when he realized what it was. The reaction of fear was instantaneous. He didn't know he could jump so high or run so fast. Everywhere he went, all the humps of snow turned out to be more bears. For some reason, they weren't interested in him that much. Still, he ran.

He lay there, waiting for the bears to settle down. He quickly realized the other scent he smelled was the bear scent. *I'd better remember that scent,* thought Nu.

The reason the bears were not interested in me was because the bears were full of the fish blubber. They probably couldn't run more than few steps! After that realization, Nu gathered enough courage to again approach the large fish, this time from the other side. There were no bears nearby. He started to feast. The blubber tasted really good. He felt his strength coming back with each bite. That was a big fish. He realized that there would be enough food for many days to come. He didn't overeat, which was a wise choice. He went around the slumbering bears and up the rocks nearby. He found a good spot between two giant rocks. He knew the bears couldn't get him there. He spent the next two days feasting on the carcass and sleeping.

After the feast over the last few days, Nu has stored a lot of fat. He was ready to go to the next island. He started running on the flat snow again. The short daylight was replaced by the long night. As he run, Nu searched for the long lights. Before the sun rose again, he found the next long light. He started running toward it.

The sun just started rising when Nu got to the next structure. This time he didn't find any humans or dogs. Nu decided to explore the shore for more big dead fish. Nu was almost on the other side when he picked up the scent of a dead seal. He started running toward it. He found the seal. Some parts of it were missing, but Nu didn't care. He ate most of the seal. He remembered the delicious taste of the intestines and fat. He gobbled those bits up, but he left some for breakfast. After his meal, he looked for shelter. He decided to sleep under snow, and he slept well.

In the morning he woke up, stretched, and shook off the snow. He went to finish off the seal, and then continued running.

Island Hopping Aleutian Style Part 2

Nu ran on the flat snow. He felt the cool wind on his pelt. As he run he looked for food. The night came fast, and soon, Nu was using moonlight to see. In the middle of the night Nu found another seal carcass. Somebody had cut the seal open and taken most of it away, but the person left the skin and the blubber behind. Nu was happy he found a meal. He ate fast before bears could smell it. Since there was no place to find shelter, he ran some more, hoping that he could find a place to rest soon. The day came, and still, there were no shelter in sight. Nu's full belly slowed him down. He was tired and sleepy, and he decided to lay on the snow and rest. It wasn't as cold as when it was nighttime. He slept through the

The Tale Of Nu

day. The moon was up again, illuminating the snow around him. Nu ran for the rest of the night. At the crack of dawn, he heard a loud noise, but it was a familiar sound. Up in the distance, he saw some faint lights. They were moving slowly. As he approached, he realized that the flat ground was being replaced by water.

The water stretched as far as his eyes could see. He became very confused. That was something he didn't expect. He remembered his grandfather's advice to always avoid open water, so he stayed on the snow, looking for a safe way to get to the other side. He ran away from the sun all day. At nightfall, he saw a long light. Then land appeared. He tried to approach the long light, but he couldn't. There was no way to get to it. There was only water between him and the structure with the long light. Being unable to pay the long light a visit, Nu pressed on, always running on the snow, but never too far from the water. That night, Nu saw a thing he had never seen before. On the far right from him, he observed the moon. All of a sudden, some kind of weird moving lights appeared to the left of him. They were flickering as if they were made by some big candle. He appreciated what he saw because it broke the darkness. *This is pretty*, he thought. And he saw more land too. It didn't seem like anyone lived there. There was no smoke, no scent of any kind. Nu decided just to press forward.

Nu started getting hungry. He couldn't even think of how many days and nights he'd been running. He was depleting the energy from the last meal rapidly. He thought about the last stop, how he slept during daytime. It became clear that sleeping during daytime and running at night was a better choice. Since the night wasn't as dark as usual, he spied land to his right. He approached it, and found a small shelter. There he curled up, and slept. He slept for a long time. It was well into the night when he woke up. He continued running, trying to be alert for any opportunity for an easy meal. There was nothing on the ground, and he couldn't smell any food, so he kept running. He passed land that had a lot of inviting but strange lights. Also, a lot of weird and scary noises came from the area, so he decided not to give it a try. At this point, he felt really weak. His stomach had been empty for a long time. His muscles were cramping too. Nu had never had this happen to him before, and he didn't know what was happening with his body. He lay down on some rocks and fell asleep.

Divine Intervention

"How's our pup doing on his journey?" The Great Canine in the Sky asked, but he didn't like the answer.

"He's not doing well, your Holiest of the Holy. He's had nothing to eat for five days. He's completely starved and exhausted, and I don't see any food for him for miles around. I'm afraid that our pup has reached the end of his journey on this Earth."

"I can't have that! I told you to assist him on this journey!"

"Yes, Your Holiness, I remember your orders."

"Then do it! Now!" ordered The Great Canine in the Sky.

A large seal pup was resting inside his hole in the ice, close to the rocks where Nu slept. All of a sudden, his ice-shelter started shaking, and then seal pup thought he saw a mouth filled with sharp teeth. Panicked, he sprang out of his lair and started scooting toward the jagged rocks, grunting with fear.

All that commotion woke Nu up. He saw the seal get stuck between two jagged rocks until it couldn't move any more. Nu had never killed a seal before. He disposed of some rabbits, but not a seal. The hunger pains in his grumbling tummy woke his predatory instincts. He sprang toward the seal. Instinctively he knew what he had to do. He ate as much as he could. He was glad he finally had something to eat. Again, he remembered his grandfather's advice that he should eat anything he could find on the flat ground. He thought about the possibility of bears smelling the seal carcass, but he was so full that he didn't feel like doing anything about it. He just found another shelter and went to sleep. When he woke up, he went searching for his seal carcass and found it where he had left it. He was grateful the bears hadn't come to visit. Nu had to finish the seal. He ate more until he couldn't eat another bite. He never wondered what had caused the seal to appear so close to where he was resting. He was just happy that the seal had been there.

As the night chased the day away, he ate the last of the seal blubber and flesh, and then he continued on his journey.

Island hopping Aleutian-Style Continues

He ran all night without stopping, he felt strong as if he had no worries in his life. Everything seemed effortless. *It makes a big difference, having food in your stomach,* thought Nu. As he ran, his mind started to wander back to his village, his mom and dad, the humans, and his grandfather. He wondered if his journey would have been easier if his grandfather had come with him. As the night progressed, clouds covered the moon. It got very dark really fast. Even though he couldn't see that much, he could rely on his hearing, so he pressed on. At the end of the night, it started to snow. Running on the fresh snow felt better. Even though the visibility was improving, it still didn't do much for Nu. The snowfall was getting heavier and heavier. As he kept running, he started hearing a rumbling sound to his right. It was the same kind of sound he had heard when he had started his journey. He knew there was some sort of big village where humans resided, and he decided not to inquire. His belly was full, his energy high, and there was no reason to look for food. He continued to run in the low visibility.

As the morning came, he spotted some land pultruding from the flat ground. He decided to rest there. This land didn't rise too high. He came upon a small hill, and he raced up to the top of it. On both sides, there were big rocks. He was curious. He wanted to explore. Animal tracks in the snow piqued his curiosity. He decided to sleep first and explore later.

When he woke up, he felt that he could have something to eat. He wasn't starving. He still had plenty of energy left, so he followed the rabbit tracks that he had discovered. He dug out a bunny from his lair and ate it. For some reason he let out a loud bark. Snow around him became alive with fleeing rabbits. He chased and caught another and another. *My goodness*, he thought, *this place is full with food!* He spent the night and another day there eating and resting. During the next night he decided to explore some more. To his surprise, he even saw a few bushes. They were covered by snow, but still, they were bushes. Finally, he reached the other side of the high ground, and he spied flat land again. He thought about staying. Somehow, he knew this could be his land of plenty if not his final destination.

The moon gave him an idea about which way to continue

his voyage. And he pressed on. The night was quiet, and again, there was nothing around him to break the monotony of the flat ground. He ran at a steady pace. The night turned into day and then back to night. Nu was passing by different kinds of lands. Some were small hills. Others were tall mountains. None of it appealed to Nu. His stomach was still digesting the rabbits, and he didn't feel like stopping. He just kept running. On the third night, he came upon something that was somewhat different. There was a long mountain to the right. He changed his direction and started running toward it. He saw a structure with a long light, but to his disappointment, it seemed that no one was there. The ground was rocky, but it wasn't like the other lands he had seen before. In some places the ground rose gently from the flat land. He thought about exploring it, but there weren't any animal tracks either. From his experience he knew there might not be any food, so he kept moving. He ran all night almost until the sun started peeking from the horizon. Then he spotted some lights. They weren't that bright and weren't as plentiful as he had seen before. He knew it was a small village. He hoped it was similar to the one he had left. Then suddenly, the flat land stopped, and the water took over the horizon. He moved on to the beach and continued to run toward the village. By this time, the sun was high in the sky, shining upon the village in front of him. There were many boats, and humans around. He liked it that way.

  The smell of fish was overwhelming, he kept crisscrossing the beach area but there was nothing to eat, just a bunch of wet small rocks and nothing else. All that pungent smell made

Nu hungry. Finally, Nu went into the village. There was still nothing to eat. All his senses were overwhelmed. After a short while, he reached the other side of the village. There was a huge structure. Humans were constantly going in and out, bringing all kinds of fish in and coming out empty-handed. He saw many seagulls flying above this place. He knew that where the seagulls were, there was food too. He trotted to the other side of the building, and there it was. All types of fish parts lying all over the place. The ground was literally covered with fish scraps and creatures trying to eat them. Nu joined the feast. He ate until he couldn't eat anymore. He realized that he should spend some more time in this place. Even though the snow was everywhere, the warmth coming from the buildings felt good. He decided to find shelter nearby. He stayed in the village for the next few days and nights.

He felt good. He had tons of energy. His belly was full, and he was ready to continue on his voyage. On his last day at the fishing village, he filled up on fish as much as he could eat. Then he took off again. It was hard to get out of this place. On the sunny side was the open ocean. On the other were rugged mountains. Eventually, he managed to find the flat ground again. He felt strong. He ran relentlessly. There were many villages on both sides of the flat ground. The village lights were the only things that broke the white monotony of the snow. At the beginning he ran, ignoring the temptations of food. At some places the open water broke up the monotony of the flat land. There were fishing boats and other water structures that he ran by. Two days and two nights came and went after

The Tale Of Nu

he left the fishing village. Nu thought that he should look for some more food again. Between him and the villages was open water. He couldn't go that way, so he turned to his right. Up in the distance, there were lights. He decided to go in that direction.

Soon after the flat land open up to water, so he was forced to embark upon the nearest solid land. Nu found that the beach wasn't as rocky as others. When Nu went inland, he ran on the packed snow, which easily carried him. When he reached the village, it was the same scene as the one he had seen before. There were plenty of fishing boats, similar structures, the same smell, the same noises, and the seagulls screeching in the air. It was confusing to Nu because he thought that he was in the same place as before. Somehow, he knew this was different. He approached the village like it was his own. This time he knew where to find the food, and he quickly found what he was looking for.

Again, the fish parts were everywhere. The seagulls were there as expected. Smaller dogs and even some foxes were feasting, and Nu eagerly joined them. He spent a few days eating as much food as he could, and sleeping the rest of the time. Again, the thought about staying there crossed his mind. The food was plentiful. It wasn't as cold as the other places on his journey. But at the beginning of his journey, he said he would go the land of endless doggie biscuits, and this wasn't it. Finally, he decided to leave the village.

Instinctively, he headed in the direction of the rising sun. The view was always the same. On one side was the open water. On the other, he saw the rugged mountains. He spent the whole day searching for a passage. He even thought of swimming for it, but at the first touch of the water, he knew he wouldn't survive if he tried. Finally, he remembered how he got on this piece of land, and he headed back. The way back took him back to the village. He took advantage of the free meal and the plentiful shelters again. As the morning came, he ate some more, and then he ran in the opposite direction. Finally, he found the snow-covered flat land. He chose to run near the open water as he always did before.

He ran a whole day and a whole night. Just before the sun came up he saw a strange glow in the sky straight ahead. The spectacle was very unusual. The faint glow was getting stronger as he approached it. A short distance away, he realized the lights were coming from a huge village he'd never seen before. There were many noisy creatures, flying in and out of the village. He was wondering what he should do next. Then he remembered his grandfather's advice to go around big villages instead of through them. Nu decided to go to his left this time.

On Solid Ground Once Again

Nu headed in the direction where there were no lights. He wondered if he made the correct decision. There were more flying creatures above him, and sometimes the noise was unbearable. He thought that he was lucky they weren't interested in him. As the sky became brighter, he realized that on the other side of the human populated area were very tall mountains. He was very confused. He didn't feel like climbing any mountains, so he pressed on with his plan to travel in the direction from where the sun came up. Soon after, he ran on top of a large hill. What he saw below was something he had never seen before, and it scared him. First, there was a river and then a really wide path with many horseless carriages on it. Some were small. Some were bigger, and some were huge! He had no idea how to cross these new obstacles. He didn't know if he should even try. Then he remembered his grandfather's advice to always travel on the wide paths when he could.

He didn't want to be disrespectful of his grandfather's advice, but surely, grandpa hadn't seen this one. This path was impossible to traverse. He had to find another way to continue. Instinctively, he knew not to leave the river. He decided to travel upriver, the only question was if he should run on the snow or on the riverbed. The dry part of the riverbed was covered by sand. Running in the sand brought back the memories of the old days when he ran with his mom and dad on the beach. As the hunger started creeping up, he started to pay attention in order to find some food. This sand was not like the beach. The riverbed was void of anything edible. No fish, no crustaceans, no shells, nothing! Nu approached the running water and peered in it. He didn't see any fish swimming, but perhaps the water was too deep. He continued running on the riverbed. At this time of year, the river was running half empty. At one point the river went under the wide path. Nu thought about taking some shelter, but the noise of the carriages running above him was too loud. He knew he couldn't sleep there. Once on the other side of the path, he realized he could use the light that the carriages made to see the area better.

At the first crack of dawn, he approached another village. The whole place was lit up unlike anything he'd seen before. He climbed up the hill and approached the village cautiously.

The Tale Of Nu

This is a very small place, he thought. *I like the lights. I hope there is some food.* The whole place was full of horseless carriages. Most of them didn't move. They were all around the big structure in the middle. There were a lot of good sounds and smells coming from it too. Nu's instinct told him to stay away from it. So he started circling it.

At the darkest side, he found some strange large boxes. The scent coming from the boxes wasn't appealing, but obviously, there was food in them. This time Nu wisely decided to inquire. He approached the boxes carefully. As he came closer; his hunger overcame his caution. He found all kinds of food, something edible he couldn't identify, bread and best of all, lots of bones. There were more bones to chew on than he had ever seen before. He took advantage of the surplus, and he ate until he was full. He took some bones in his mouth and went back to the riverbed. He found a small shelter and curled up in it and started chewing on his bone. He felt safer there. Exhausted from his long run, he finally fell asleep with a bone resting on the side of his snout.

In the morning he went to the river for a drink. Drinking that water made Nu feel refreshed. It reminded him of drinking in his old village. It tasted better than eating snow. When he quenched his thirst, he decided to go back to the spot of last night's feast. He filled up on bread and some other goodies. Lastly, he took the biggest bone he could find and started his journey once again. This time he was running between the road and the river. He thought that was much better idea than what he did last time.

As the night was approaching, to his surprise, he discovered the river was flowing from different direction that the path. Also, the path had seemed to shrink. It was smaller than before. The carriages were not as plentiful as they had been either. He decided to follow the narrower path and abandon the river. Nu didn't know that following the path was the right choice. All he knew was to follow his grandfather's advice. Nu passed by farms and other houses. He saw animals that looked like they had branches in their head, while others were smaller. This was a new world to him. Sometimes, Nu would stop and look around. Sometimes, he would only sniff the air because there were strange scents coming from the farms. He was curious but didn't inquire. He just pressed on.

Before the end of the day, Nu saw a building that seemed abandoned. He approached the structure and confirmed that it was uninhabited. He went inside and made himself at home. As soon as he settled down, he heard a lot of commotion. That place was crawling with rats. *Oh, great,* thought Nu. *I won't have to work hard for my breakfast!* He fell asleep very fast. When he woke up he immediately started chasing rats. He caught three and ate them right away. It seemed that wasn't enough. He was still hungry, so he caught some more! After he satisfied his hunger, he decided to go back to his trail.

When he was just about to continue on his way by the path, he saw something that completely made him stop in awe. Right in front of him stood a large animal. It was larger than anything that he had seen before, other than the dead fish. And it had branch-like things coming out of its head.

The Tale Of Nu

Nu didn't know either to be afraid or not. Soon, he became anxious and started barking. The animal in front of him suddenly jumped and started running away. Nu wasn't going to give chase. He just stood there. *I guess I scared them, didn't I,* thought Nu. *I wonder what they are, and what was that voice that came out of me? It was loud and ferocious, wasn't it?* He continued on his path. At one point the path split in two. Some horseless carriages went right, and some went left. In front of him was a tall mountain. *Which way to go? Which way to go?* He repeated the question to himself. He could take either path. He didn't want to meet any horseless carriages. So finally, he took the right path since that way seemed to be less dangerous.

The forest to the right was getting thicker. Again, everything was covered in white. Hill after hill, it was all the same. Sometimes the mountains were closer to him. Other times they were farther away. One time he came upon a river that was covered by ice and snow. He had to cross it, because he didn't want any obstacles between him and the path the horseless carriages took. He already knew that the paths were the easiest way to travel.

After it got dark, he could even run on the path because he could see the carriages from far away and could yield to them in time. He enjoyed the opportunity to run at a steady speed. Sometimes he would run higher than the path and observe the surrounding nature. Other times he could see animals drinking from the stream. He pressed on and didn't bother stopping at the first village that he saw. He ran around it and then continued onward. Soon he reached another village, and he didn't bother stopping again. He could sometimes hear the barking of village dogs, but that didn't entice him to stop ether. He pressed on. Somehow, he knew this area was not the final destination of his journey.

After a while, he noticed something strange. All the horseless carriages were going in the same direction as he was. None was coming from the other side, and he wondered why. He continued running. Soon, he noticed all the horseless carriages had stopped. Nothing was moving on the path. Finally, he arrived at yet another village. This village was totally littered with stopped horseless carriages. Some had humans in them, and some didn't. *Something must be going on*, Nu thought. Again, he ran around the settlement. He found the path again and continued running away from the village.

Not far from the village, he heard a lot of strange noises. The loud sound was echoing around the canyon he just entered. Soon after, he discovered what the noise was. Right in front of him was a tall snow hill. It covered the path and the stream and made everything impossible. There were all sorts of lights on these gigantic machines trying to move the snow. He realized he couldn't climb over the snow hill, so he decided to wait for the humans to clear the path. The work progress was slow. Nu decided to go back to the village and look for shelter and maybe some food. He went back to the big area where the horseless carriages had stopped. This place was full of noise. Most of the horseless carriages were spewing clouds of smoke, and Nu discovered when he got close to them, the air got warmer. He found a particularly large horseless carriage, and he discovered it was emitting heat. Nu gathered enough courage to crawl underneath it, and he felt it was warm indeed. He got used to the noise and fell asleep.

In the morning just out of boredom, he started looking for food. He cautiously approached the structure in the middle. Finally, he caught a familiar scent. He headed in that direction. He knew where he could find food and eat. Once he had his fill he decided to explore his surroundings. He went out of the village, unsure of what he was looking for and what he'd find. Finally, he came upon an area that was completely undisturbed. There were no tracks in the snow. He started rolling on his back, trying to clean his coat. The clean snow felt good. Once he was finished grooming, he started looking around. He was almost above the tree line. He could easily see the top of the village structures, and he smelled the smoke from the chimneys. It was much quieter up there. After a night spent under a noisy horseless carriage, the quiet felt good. He was wondering what to do next. Should he stay, or should he continue on his journey? He decided to see how much of the snow the humans had dug up.

This time he stayed high up by the tree line. Soon, he got to the point of where the sliding snow had taken all the trees all the way down to the path. From up there, he could easily see that it was possible for him to cross to the other side, and he did just that. He thought about his lack of breakfast. He could go back to the last village. After all, he wasn't that far from it. But he decided to go forward. It seemed like the villages were not as scarce anymore. After he crossed the area of fallen snow, he saw the path again. This time it was lined up with horseless carriages pointing to the other direction. He thought about going down to the path, but he decided to stay near the tree line.

His progress was slower, and a short while later, the sun fell behind the mountain. Nu thought that the day was almost over and figured that traveling near the tree line in the dark was dangerous, so he went back down to the path. Most of the humans were inside of their carriages. Some of them were out. When the humans saw Nu approach, they got out of his way by going inside their horseless carriages. They seemed scared of him. Nu wondered why, but he didn't stick around to find out. It didn't appear to him that he had grown to be a really big dog, almost as big as his father. Humans on the path had never seen a creature like him. They didn't know what to make of him. Nu pressed on.

Just at the end of daylight, he came up to another fork in the road. Nu stopped, not knowing which way to go. He looked to the right. There was nothing in that direction to awaken his curiosity. He looked to the left. And he saw some faint glow. From his own experience, that glow can come from a human village. His hunger was telling him to go left. He crossed the path easily since there were no carriages in sight. Soon after that he came upon the lights. He looked to his left, and he found out the lights were in a perfect line leading away from the path. Nu didn't know what to make of it. It seemed like there were no humans in the area. Nu couldn't figure out why. *If there are no humans, then there is no food!* He concluded.

He was running quite fast on the empty path. Light snow started to fall. He hoped the snow would stop soon. He didn't like traveling when it was snowing. Finally, he reached another village. It seemed like it was late when he arrived. The main structure was dark, and Nu couldn't see any humans. There were many horseless carriages parked everywhere. Before he could think of resting, he knew he should find some food. It was harder to find a scent when it was snowing, but he got lucky. He knocked down some boxes to get to the food inside, and that made a lot of noise. Nu looked around, hoping nobody heard anything. It seemed like all the humans were fast asleep. He ate quickly. The scraps were not as plentiful as they had been at the last stop. He found a bone, and he gladly took it. Then he headed to find a shelter under the nearest horseless carriage. After he was done gnawing on his bone, he fell asleep.

He was startled by a great noise that came from above. At first, he didn't know what was going on. He crawled out from under the horseless carriage and ran away, and he ran just in time because the carriage started moving. *Whew,* thought Nu, *he almost ran me over. I have to be more careful.* At that thought he went back to the box, looking for some more food. After he finished his meal, he chose to continue on his journey until he realized the snow from the previous night had covered his tracks. He couldn't figure out where he had come in from. He wasn't sure which way to go. He decided to follow the tracks of the horseless carriage that he had slept under. He stayed on the path for a very long time, stopping briefly to drink from the occasional streams. There weren't any carriages coming from behind him. *Maybe they didn't clear the snow yet.* He didn't miss yielding to the carriages when they passed. He quickened his pace.

At the height of the day, he approached a village. Many humans lived there. He could tell by all the clouds coming out of their structures. Right by the path and next to a flowing river, there was a structure from which the scent of cooked meat emanated, overwhelming Nu's senses. He wasn't that hungry, but he couldn't resist the possibility of a good meal. He approached the box with the strongest scent. He knew that there was food inside. There was a lot of meat on the bones he found. He began digging into his newly discovered loot, and he ate until he couldn't eat anymore. Then he took off again. This time he stayed close to the little river, knowing that he would need to drink. Nu covered a lot of ground. Even though the days were shorter than the nights, Nu felt more refreshed and stronger when he slept at night.

Slowly, the view opened up. He was entering another valley. This one was so large he couldn't even see the mountains that cradled it. All of a sudden, he became disoriented. Traveling through the mountains made it easy to go in one direction. Now that advantage was gone. The air coming from his right had a faint smell of the sea. He decided to stay on the path as usual, but he didn't want the view of the mountains to go. He thought that his destiny rested near the sea.

Just before sundown, the path led him to a spot that was quite curious and confusing to Nu. Many symbols hung from

The Tale Of Nu

a bunch of tall branchless trees. They were different shapes and shades. He didn't know what to make of it. In the middle of the path, there was a structure with smoke rising from the top of it. He knew there were humans inside. This time there were no other dogs around. He decided not to disturb anybody, so he kept running. He decided to stay at the first village he found. It took him sometime to get to the first village. When he arrived there, it was late and dark. He was more tired than hungry, so he searched for shelter first. This time he took shelter between two small structures not far from the path.

Soon after he discovered his shelter, it started snowing quite heavily. He wasn't concerned with the snow. The shelter he had chosen protected him well. He had no idea how long he slept. When he finally woke up, he couldn't see anything. It was completely dark. He became disoriented. He didn't know what to make of the predicament he was in. He started moving inside the confined area. He tried to dig his way out, but he couldn't do it. That side was solid. Then he tired a different direction with the same results. Finally, his nose touched something wet and cold. He realized it was snow, and he started digging franticly. He made quick progress, and the hole opened. He realized that his shelter was covered in snow. He crawled out of the hole and found that the snow was falling strong. He thought about going back inside his shelter, but the rumbling from his stomach forced him to search for food. He crawled outside and started looking for something to eat.

Everything was covered by snow. His nose led him to a box buried in snow. He knew there was food inside. Getting inside the box and to find the food was going to be difficult. When he was trying to find a way into the box, a human came out of the nearest structure carrying something big. He dropped his load outside the box, and he ran back to the structure. Nu left his hiding place and went to the box to sniff around. Whatever the human brought out of the structure had food inside. Nu couldn't believe his luck. He ate for a long time. Everything he ate was delicious. Finally, he grabbed some scraps and took them to his shelter. He knew he couldn't travel in conditions like this. He was forced to stay there for many days.

Yukon Bound

Nu completely lost track of how long he was waiting for the snowstorm to pass. He divided the time between eating scraps and sleeping. After a long while, Nu realized that he'd better leave. It was still snowing, but it was tolerable. After a little while, the moon came out of the clouds and washed the ground with a silver glow. Running again felt good after all those days he spent in a small shelter.

He ran for a whole night. After a while, he came up on some flat land covered by snow. Behind it were some big mountains. The flat land reminded him of his journey not that long ago. He appreciated the idea that if something happened on the path, he could always run on the flat land. As the lights started to creep up from the left and started rising higher, he started running faster. He knew in the daytime there will be more horseless carriages on the path. The day broke. Sunlight raced across the ground. He found out the path approached the mountains to his left. To his left and all up the mountain, there were trees that were charred black, without any foliage. They looked the same as the pieces of wood that humans would put on an open fire. Nu wondered what type of disaster happened to the forest. At this point, the flat ground was on his left side.

He kept running for a very long distance. He saw the same burned trees to his right and the flat snow-covered land on the left. At this point, the snow that was covering the path started melting off. Running on the melting snow was a completely different experience for him. Running on melting snow was not something he enjoyed. He even thought about abandoning the path altogether. Fortunately, that wasn't a problem much longer. Nu found the path began to dry out. The snow was on the sides only. This made the travel easier. He was covering more ground, and his feet felt better when he was running on warm land.

At the end of the day, he came upon another human village. Before he got into the village, he saw to his left a single rugged structure. It reminded him of a few shelters that he has chosen before. He approached it carefully and looked from every side to make sure nobody was in it. He went inside just as night was falling.

Just as soon as he went inside, he picked up the scent of rats and other animals. He knew that he had chosen wisely. He chose the warmest corner he could find and curled up. The morning brought the familiar sound of tiny feet running all over the place. He knew this sound. He opened his eyes and saw an almost endless amount of rats moving around. He rose to his feet, stretched, licked his chops, and started hunting. There were so many rats that for every leap he made, he caught one. This barn was unreal. He ate many rats, and then he hunted some more and ate more. Finally, it was time to move on. The whole floor was littered with rat feet and tails. Those were the parts that Nu hated to eat. As before, the idea of staying crossed his mind, but he knew that this area was not the place where his journey would end.

He exited the barn. Just on the other side of the nearby path, he heard a bubbling sound which reminded him of his thirst. The water was sweet and cold, he enjoyed his drink. Once he filled up, he continued up stream. He never even came close to the human village. Soon after, he saw the path again. He liked what he saw, a path with a creek on its side.

The Ride

Nu followed the wide path, stopping only to rest, drink, or eat. Nu ran for a bit when he found another structure. He was very tempted to inquire what was inside but he decided to keep on running till the night came. After the nightfall, it turned very cold. Heavy snow fell and there were no lights in sight. Short while after he saw a very large horseless carriage on the side of the wide path. Nu crawled under it and curled up.

The driver saw Nu go under the truck. He was just parked there, waiting out the snowstorm. The man hated driving in snowstorms, even though he would make more money if he drove through it. Time was literally money. Besides, the longer he stayed on the this road, he would lose more valuable time with his family. He thought about bringing Nu with him. The dog would keep him company, and his older dog at home would enjoy a friend, although it would mean spending more money on food. *But then, that dog could help protect us,* he thought.

    Nu woke up under the horseless carriage. He was hungry. In fact, he was starving. It was as bad as that one time on the flat ground. He got up from under the horseless carriage. He shook his fur and stretched. He decided to see if there was a human in the carriage. Nu started to bark loudly at the large carriage.

    The man woke up. There was a loud noise outside his truck, and he openned the truck door to see what was causing the racket. He saw the dog again. It looked starved. He went back in to get the garbage bag and threw down some of his leftovers. The dog gobbled them up and then looked back up, waging its tail. The man threw down little more food and then put some on the seat next to him. Then he opened the passenger door.

    Nu saw him put the scraps in the horseless carriage. *It's better in there than out here!* Nu thought . So he climbed into the horseless carriage, and the human shut the door. The driver got inside the carriage with him, and the carriage started to move. Nu almost choked on his food. He definitely didn't expect this to happen. The fear that he felt was paralyzing. All he could do was lie on the floor and close his eyes. Nu felt every bump and move of the carriage. After a while, he started to realize that maybe the carriage didn't pose any immediate threats. He had no idea where they were or where they were going.

He was still on the floor when the carriage stopped. The human got out of the carriage. As he walked away, Nu realized he was surrounded by a sort of quietness. There was no sound of any kind, and nothing was moving. He gathered some courage and looked outside of the carriage's window. There were some structures around and many other carriages everywhere he looked. Snow was still falling, but not as hard as before.

After a while, the human came out of one of the structures, carrying something with him, and then he got back inside the carriage. Nu could smell many different scents. They all smelled good to him. The human got something out of the bag and offer it to Nu. It was a huge bone. Nu started barking loudly. He was excited, and he accepted the offer. M*aybe this is a good human*, he thought to himself. He lay on the floor and gnawed on his bone. He was so busy working on his bone that he didn't notice that the carriage started moving again. This time Nu didn't feel any fear. Then the human started talking to him. Needless to say, Nu didn't understand a word he said. "How's that bone, boy?" asked the human "That's a bone from a White Horse" he said jokingly. "You don't get my joke, do you?" The man continued, "I had hoped that this snow would let up so we could go faster." This time Nu looked at him. He looked back at Nu and petted him. Nu felt good. He was warm and rested. He felt safe, and he wasn't hungry. Life was good. By nightfall, the snow subsided.

Once they got out of the snowy area, travel became much easier and faster. It was interesting experience to Nu, being inside the carriage versus having to yield every time they

The Tale Of Nu

approached him. Up in the distance, there was some type of glow in the dark sky. "You see that light, buddy?" the human asked. "That is Prince George. I think I'm gonna name you Prince George. Yup, that's a good name for you. You're a big dog, and your dad must have been a king of all dogs. I could have named you White Horse because we met there, but I don't think White Horse is a good name for a dog, don't you agree?" Nu didn't understand a thing, but to show his appreciation, he wagged his tail. When they got to the outskirts of the big city, Nu appreciated the lights from inside of the carriage. It was almost the same as the view at the beginning of his journey. The human stopped the carriage and got out. He wasn't gone for long though. When he came back, he put something around Nu's neck and said, "Buddy, I have to put this around your neck. People won't let me walk you without it. I hope you understand." He patted his head. The gesture made all of Nu's fear go away. When they got out of the horseless carriage, Nu realized that he had to do his business. They walked besides each other like they had known each other for all of their lives. When Nu was finished, they went back to the carriage and got back inside.

Moving Real Fast

When they woke up and got out of the carriage, the sun was already up. After a short walk, Nu saw on the side of the carriage something that seemed familiar. The length of the carriage displayed many stars and many stripes. This sight brought Nu a lot of pleasure, and reassurance that he had made the right decision about this human, his new friend. His human friend pulled some meat from a box inside of the carriage and started burning it. The smell of meat filled the inside of the carriage and drove Nu crazy. It excited all his senses. He couldn't stop drooling, and the force of his wagging tail pushed everything that it touched. The human ate and gave pieces of his food to Nu. He was happy. Then the human noticed that it wasn't enough, so he pulled out a bag, pulled out some rocks, and offered them to Nu. Nu sniffed them. They smelled like food, so he ate them.

The Tale Of Nu

Once the human cleaned up the inside of the carriage, they moved on. This time they traveled at much faster speed than before, and they covered a lot of ground. Nu wasn't used to the speed. He couldn't even see what was on the side of the path, so he concentrated on the mountains, the woods and the river that they traveled next to. The view was changing rapidly. "I'll tell you, buddy, before the end of the day, we're gonna be in Kelowna, weather permitting. We are gonna unload the truck and head home. You're gonna met Jack. He's a big dog like you, but he's getting old." They were going through a lot of big and small villages and at the end of the day, just before the sun set, it seemed like they arrived at their destination. The whole place seemed devoid of humans.

They drove inside an area that was all fenced in. The human stopped the carriage, got out, and went behind the big structure. When he went back to the carriage, he looked sad. "Buddy, it looks like we have to spend the night here." They walked around the carriage together. Then they ate and went to sleep.

The next day the human moved the carriage next to the structure and got out. Nu wanted to come too, but the human closed the door and left. All types of noises came from the back of the carriage. This made Nu nervous. The human came back soon after, and then they drove away. The human was talking to somebody. His voice returned to normal, which made Nu comfortable. "Buddy, we're going home. You're gonna have plenty of room to play with Jack and protect the family. Everywhere you'll look, you'll see apple trees. I hope you like apples. Do you like apples?" he said to Nu, patting his head. "You know, Buddy, we live outside of Yakima. Can you say Yakima?" The human looked at Nu, smiling. "Of course not, you're a dog. You slobbered all over my truck. When we get home, I'm gonna have to clean all this up." They drove till the sun was high up in the sky, Nu noticed that the trees were changing. They weren't only trees with tiny needles. Some of the trees looked different from the trees he was used to. Everywhere he looked there were all kinds of human villages and structures. There were many horseless carriages going in different directions. There was human activity all over the place. Nu was grateful to have his human friend with him. It seemed like they were going in the direction that Nu wanted to go in. They made some stops. Nu watched his human friend put something in the carriage. Sometimes he came back with food, and it was all good times. Nu thought about his journey. Until recently a journey that was mostly full of loneliness and peril. Before the sun went down, they got off the wide path and took a much smaller one. Everywhere he looked were trees with flowers on their brunches, bushes with leafs, and grass on the ground.

One thing that Nu wanted to see and was missing was a large body of water. Besides from a few streams and a small river, there wasn't any water to be found. *I think this is good enough for me,* Nu thought to himself. Suddenly, the horseless carriage stopped. Nu looked around, and he saw this structure nestled between two trees. As his human friend walked toward the structure, a big dog came to greet him. Nu looked

The Tale Of Nu

closer. The dog was tied up with a chain. That sight made Nu nervous. Then he remembered his grandpa and the advice he had given him never to trust a human with chains in his hand. To his horror, the human started approaching the carriage. He was dragging a long chain behind him. Nu got so nervous he peed inside the carriage. At this point, Nu had a very good idea of how he was gonna spend the rest of his life. He made the decision to run.

As the door opened, he made eye contact with the human and jumped over him. As soon as his feet touched the ground, he started running. "Hey! Where are you going?" Nu didn't even look back. With the little light left, he ran to a nearby pasture. He ducked under some fences and kept running. He had no idea where he was, where he was going, and how he was going to find shelter. All he knew was he had to get away from the human with chains. He kept running for almost the whole night. The ground was mostly flat with some sporadic trees that made for small forests. He was afraid that the human would get into his horseless carriage and give chase. Finally, he found shelter under the roots of a felled tree and he slept there.

Almost There!

The sun came up sooner than Nu expected. He was still nervous from the ordeal he had gone through last night. Nu needed to get up and run, but he didn't know where to go. Everywhere he looked were empty fields. He didn't have anything that could point him in the correct direction, nothing but the sun in the sky. So he just lay there at the edge of a small forest.

As the weather got warmer, he felt thirsty, so he knew he had to find some water. He got up and stretched. He decided to travel south in the direction of the sun. As far as he could see, there was nothing but fields and meadows. He saw some large animals eating the grass. Since they didn't bother him he wasn't paying much attention to them. Finally, he stumbled upon a small brook. After quenching his thirst, he continued chasing the sun. He was making good progress because there were no obstacles. As time passed, he encountered hills. Some were small, and some were tall. Other were covered with forests. He didn't worry much when he entered the hilly area.

At this point, he felt hungry, even though he still had energy. He found many streams that quenched his thirst. As he ran over the hills, he spotted a big rabbit, and he gave chase. This was the first time he chased an animal that wasn't running away on snow. Unfortunately, the bunny got away. He regretted wasting time and energy. He realized that when hunting on dry ground, his long, wide legs didn't carry that much of an advantage as the times when he would hunt in the snow. He realized he needed new hunting strategy. He spotted another rabbit. This time he just hid behind a bush and observed the way this rabbit behaved. He noticed that the moment the rabbit lowered his head to graze was the only advantage he could explore. Also, this rabbit's right foot was slightly in front. Nu knew from his past experiences that this rabbit will jump to his left if startled. Nu decided to give it a try at the right moment. This time he was successful in his hunt. He quickly ate his hard earned meal.

He got out of the woods, looked at the sun, and continued on his journey. Then he saw a tall hill dead ahead of him. He approached the hill and started climbing. When he reached the top of the hill, he was stunned to find a huge river flowing between him and his destination to the south. He started wondering which way he should go. Finally, he decided to follow the path of the sun. He knew he had to find the way to cross this giant obstacle.

River Crossing

Quickly, he climbed down from the hill. Between him and the river, there was a wide path. From his previous experience, he knew he should travel close to the water. Even though the path was covered by carriages, he got to the other side. He felt like he wasn't scared from this moving objects like he used to be. He got to the river and drank the water. By this time, the sun was setting behind the distant mountains. Nu was following the direction that the river flowed. The noise that the horseless carriages were making was loud. He couldn't hear much of anything else. Right after the sun set, he saw a glow in the sky. He knew it had to came from a big village. Then he came upon a structure that was going over the river. He thought about crossing the river right away, but he decided to do it in the morning. He went under the structure

The Tale Of Nu

and found a good shelter to spend the night in. He felt very safe, and he fell asleep quickly.

He slept well that is until a huge noise woke him up. He was frightened like never before. He started running away like he had never run before. As he was running away, the noise subsided. At one point, he turned around to see what was going on. He saw many large strange carriages moving very slow atop the structure. He started pacing himself. Then he heard a noise from above him. He looked up, and he saw this really large bird flying above him. He had seen those birds before. He knew they weren't after him, so he kept running.

The path was getting closer to the river again. There was a noise coming from the air and the path. The river was the only safe place. This was a very noisy place, and he didn't like it, so he kept running. This much noise was overwhelming him. He had to find some quiet somewhere. He knew he had to cross the river because that was where the sun was, but he didn't know how. The riverbanks began to be hard to traverse. Sometimes they were so steep that they rose straight out of the river. He had hard time to find space to run. Progress was slow. Then he came upon a view of another structure going over the river, with carriages moving on it both ways. He ran toward it. When he reached the structure, he stood there looking in every direction. Everywhere he looked, there was a flat path covered by something black. Then he looked at the structure crossing the river. There were many paths. The carriages traveled in the middle paths. Then he saw a smaller path that nobody traveled on. It led in the direction of the sun.

He decided to go that way. It took him some time to traverse the structure.

Once he crossed the structure, the small path he traveled was going in different direction. If he had to follow the sun, he would have to follow the path that the horseless carriages used, but he didn't like that idea. The path he was on curved and headed under the structure spanning the river. He decided that was the way to go. He was at the water's edge again. At this point, there were many large birds flying overhead, making all kinds of noises. He decided to get off that path and somehow get away from the noise. To the left of him, there was a large area covered in grass and trees. He decided that was the way to go.

He finally got away from the noisy birds. He could still ear some of the roars coming from them, but it wasn't as loud and scary. Suddenly, he heard a noise that aroused his interest. Some kind of screaming was coming from the nearby grassland, and it sounded like a human in great distress. He started running toward the screams. He came to the top of a knoll and saw what was going on. There was a human trying to protect two human children from a pack of dogs. Instantly, Nu decided to help the humans. He started running as fast as he could. As he approached, the screams grew louder and louder. The dogs were getting more aggressive with the humans. Nu ran so fast that when he came upon the scene, he couldn't stop. He just plowed into the bunch of dogs, knocking every one of them off their feet. As he turned his head, he saw the alpha dog charge at the humans.

The Tale Of Nu

Nu didn't have time to gather his posture. He somehow jumped in the air, trying to get in between the humans and the alpha dog. As he was falling, he saw that the alpha dog was beneath him. He grabbed the alpha dog's snout and squeezed as hard as he could. He heard the noise of bones being broken. The alpha dog was in great pain and he gave a loud yelp. Then Nu let him go. The alpha dog ran away, followed by some of his dogs. Nu got on his feet. He stood in front of the humans, faced the rest of the pack, and started barking really loud. At that point, few carriages with all kind of scary noises and lights came from different directions. Whatever was left of the pack of dogs scattered in fear. Nu became scared too. He saw humans with sticks come out of the horseless carriages. He knew what those sticks could do. All of a sudden, the humans he was protecting came around and stood in front of him.

"Please don't shoot him," said the woman. The children were screaming too. "Don't shoot. Don't shoot!" Police officers put their guns away and approached the lady.

"Ma'am, we had a call for a dog disturbance. Is this your dog?"

She said, "Well, yes. A pack of stray dogs attacked us, and our dog saved us."

The police asked, "So are you okay?"

"Yes Sir. Just a bit scared."

The police officer asked, "Ma'am, why doesn't your dog have a tag?"

She quickly replied, "We switched the leash. The tag must have come off."

Tapping his hat the police officer said, "Please replace the tag so there are no misunderstandings. Have a great day, ma'am."

"You too, Officer," she said.

As soon as the police left the scene, the woman and her children turned to Nu. He was still scared and shaking. The woman got down on her knees and hugged the dog. Her kids were already patting the big dog.

"Mom, can we keep him? He obviously doesn't have a home."

"Baby, but he's so big!"

"Yeah," said the girl, "if he wasn't, we would have been in big trouble."

"Please, Mom? Please!" the boy pleaded. Nu instinctively knew what was going on, so he started wagging his tail.

"Okay, if he wants to go with us, we can have him."

"Yay!" celebrated the children. "We have a dog! A really big dog!" They started walking together like a big family.

Nu noticed something. The trees all around him had young wide leaves like his grandfather had told him. He had a suspicion that his journey was over, but he wasn't sure yet.

"First we have to make sure that nothing is wrong with him."

"Yes! Let's go to the vet." They reached a small horseless carriage and got inside. The humans even opened the window so he could get fresh air. The horseless carriage started moving.

The Land of Endless Doggie Biscuits

"We're gonna take him to Dr. Perkins." said the mother. "She is a good veterinarian. Her office is in downtown on Burnside Street. And then if we keep him, we're gonna have to buy him some dog food at pet shop" The children were very excited, which carried over to Nu. At this point, the dog had his head out of the car. His ears were flapping in every direction. His face was distorted by the air, and his slobber was dripping all over the road. Then they approached another river. It was smaller than the one Nu had crossed earlier that day, and there was another structure spanning the river.

As they approached the structure, Nu spotted something that he wanted to see all along. Atop of the structure was an enormous cloth with many stars and stripes on it. Nu got very excited. Finally, after all this time, he had reached the Land of the Endless Doggie Biscuits. He was there.

As they crossed the river, Nu looked all over the place to find anything that may look like a doggie biscuits. Everything was strange, and nothing looked like what he had imagined. He didn't really know what a doggie biscuit looked like. Soon, they stopped at another human structure. They all got out and went inside. Shortly after that, he was surrounded by all kinds of humans wearing white. They were all touching him in places he had never been touched before. They came to him with a machine that made Nu nervous. They cut Nu's fur and gave him a bath in nice warm water with something that smelled good. Nu felt so refreshed and happy. He never had a bath in warm water before. It was awesome. He didn't object to anything the humans did to him. He enjoyed the attention.

When it was over, his new family came in.

"How is he doing, Doctor?" the mother asked.

"You know, Mrs. Moore, I've never seen a dog like this before. Believe it or not, he is still a puppy, only a bit over a year old. He will get much bigger."

"Don't worry. We live in a house and have a large yard."

"Okay, he is healthy with only some bruises and few ticks. Nothing more than a dog collar and few pills can't fix. He doesn't have any medical issues that I could find. I gave him some pills in case he has worms. He's good to go. He seems hungry though." Children were very happy to hear the great news from the doctor.

The Tale Of Nu

"Doctor, what breed is this dog?" the mother asked the doctor.

The doctor paused for a minute. "Well, he definitely a mix. His eyes are blue like a Siberian Husky's. His fur and leg structure indicate a borzoi, but his size and the shape of the torso is something that is unknown to me. I have never seen a dog like this before, but we will find out when the blood test comes in. I will call you right away when we receive the results." The doctor gave the mother three pieces of something that looked like small bones. "You can give it to him," the doctor said. The mother offered the treats to Nu, and he ate them quickly. "Oh, and you're gonna need this," said the doctor. She gave the mother a dog collar with a name tag. "Now your dog is set," the doctor said.

They all got inside the car and drove to pet shop. When they entered the shop everyone in the store stopped what they were doing and stared at the woman, two children, and the huge dog besides them.

Many employees approached the family and started patting the big dog and asking questions. The mother informed the staff that they were looking for their largest bag of puppy food, which surprised everyone.

"Puppy food? He's still a puppy?" the employees asked.

"Yes, we need to feed him so he can grow bigger." The mother said jokingly. As they were leaving the store, they asked for help to load the goodies into the car.

At the store's exit, Nu saw the picture of a human giving his dog the same treats that he had eaten at the other structure. *Those must be doggie biscuits! Finally I made it! This is the best day of my life!* Someone was helping them load the bags in the car: a huge bag of puppy food, largest box of doggie biscuits, and the biggest bone they could find.

They all went inside the car. Soon after that, they stopped at another structure. The mother put the horseless carriage inside the structure.

"Okay, kids I need you to help me unload the station wagon"

"Yes, ma'am!" the children said obediently. The mother opened the door to the structure and let Nu in.

"Welcome home, puppy."

Nu followed her into the house.